illustrated by Frank James

Chapter 1

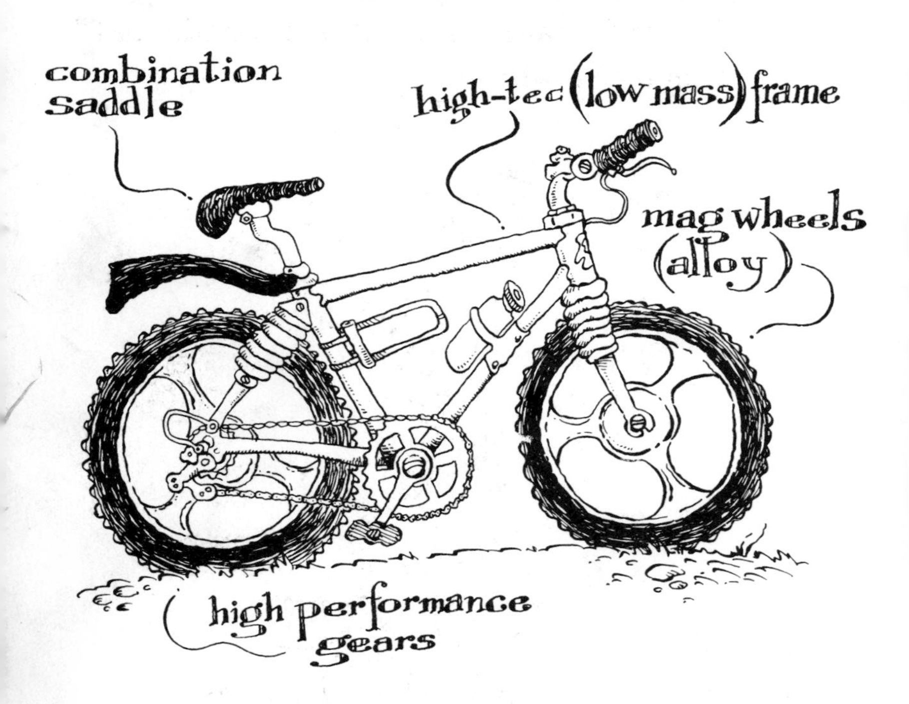

It all began on my birthday. Mum and Dad bought me a mountain bike, the Titan Supercharge Mark 1. Nothing could touch it. For six months I owned the streets. Then disaster struck. They brought out a new model, the Titan Supercharge Mark 2. Jason Percy got one. I was furious.

"Mum," I said. "I've got to have a new bike."

Mum stared at me as if I was crazy. "Alex," she said, "we've just *bought* you a new bike."

"That thing?" I said. "That's ancient!"

"Ancient?" said Mum. "It's six months old!"

"Exactly!" I said.

Mum refused to listen to reason. She said I wanted everything on a plate. She went on about the old days, when Dad had to scrimp for every penny. I pretended to yawn. Mum got really mad and sent me to my room.

Later that evening, I heard Mum and Dad talking about me. I couldn't make out much but it sounded serious. I heard Dad's fist coming down on the table and the word "lesson".

I had a nasty feeling Dad wasn't talking about school.

Next morning, a big red delivery van came up our road.

"What do you know?" I said to myself. "They've got me the bike after all!"

I waited for the doorbell. It didn't ring. I peeked out through the curtains. The delivery

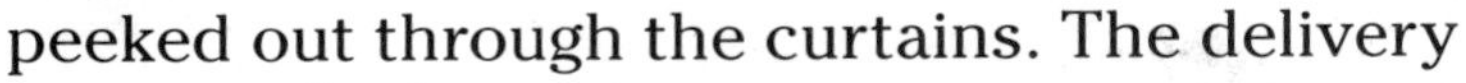

van was reversing back up the road.

That's funny, I thought to myself.

I went out. There was no package on the doorstep. All I saw was a boy about my age, sitting on our garden wall.

"Are Mr and Mrs Tucker at home?" asked the boy.

"No," I replied.

"May I come in and wait for them?" he asked.

I shrugged. "I suppose so," I replied.

The boy breezed past me into the house. There was a faint smell of disinfectant about him. He walked straight through to the living-room and sat down.

"Well, Alex," he said, "this *is* a nice place."

"How do you know my name?" I asked.

The boy winked and tapped his nose. "I'm Mark, by the way," he said. "Mark Two."

"Mark Two?" I said. "What kind of name is that?"

"It's not really a *name*," he replied. "More of a description."

Mark Two held out his hand. I shook it. It was rather cool, and very clean, with the nails cut into perfect semicircles.

"May I have a look round?" said Mark Two suddenly.

I didn't really know what to say. Not that it mattered, because Mark Two was already strolling round the room, admiring the family photos. He then decided on a tour of the hall. I followed close behind, in case he tried to nick something.

"I can find my own way, thank you," said Mark Two. He went off up the stairs. I listened anxiously as his soft shoes padded about. Doors opened and closed. Taps went on and off. Mark Two came back down.

"Tell me, Alex," he said. "Which is your room?"

This was going too far. “My room,” I said, “is my business.”

“Oh, I’m sorry,” said Mark Two. “I didn’t realize you had something to hide.”

Mark Two looked at me with a challenge in his eyes. His eyes were blue, like mine, except his were deeper. Come to that, his nose was like mine, except straighter. His mouth was quite similar too, but none of the teeth had fillings.

I was starting to dislike Mark Two.

“I’ve got nothing to hide,” I told him.

We went up to my room. Mark Two wandered coolly inside. His eyes roved past the Manchester City poster, the scattered video games and the dirty socks. He didn't say anything about the smell, but as soon as my back was turned, he opened a window.

"Is this your bed?" he asked, testing the springs.

"That's right," I said. "*My* bed."

Mark Two sat down on it. "Very comfy," he said. "Gosh, I'm thirsty!"

"Maybe you'd like some of *my* Ribena," I said, sarcastically.

"That would be lovely," replied Mark Two.

Gritting my teeth, I went down and fetched Mark Two some Ribena. When I got back he was face down on the bed and fast asleep.

old sock
homework
records
WHAT

MAN CITY F.C.
Very smelly
Laundry

Mum and Dad were not at all surprised when I told them about the strange boy.

"That'll be Mark Two," said Mum.

"How did you know?" I asked.

Mum and Dad went up to inspect the sleeping boy. "Yes, that's Mark Two all right," said Dad.

"Lovely clean hair," said Mum.

"What are we going to do with him?" I demanded.

Dad thought for a moment. "There's an air-bed in the cupboard," he said.

"That's *my* air-bed," I moaned. "He's not sleeping on it!"

"Quite right," said Dad. "You are."

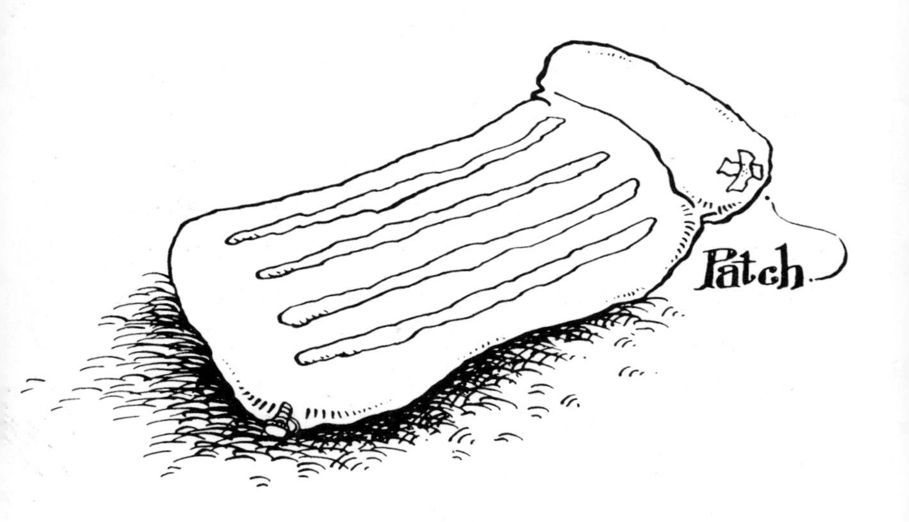

Chapter 2

Next morning I woke to the sound of crunching. Mark Two was sitting up in bed munching a bowl of cornflakes. On the floor beside him were two suitcases.

"Good morning," he said, cheerily. "Do help yourself to breakfast."

I decided to ignore him. Eventually he was sure to go away. I threw on some clothes and went out for a kickabout with my mates. An hour or two later, when I came back, Mark Two was busily folding his trousers and hanging them in my wardrobe.

"Make yourself at home," I said, sarcastically.

"Thank you," he replied.

Lunchtime arrived, and Mark Two still showed no signs of leaving. An alarm clock had appeared on my dressing-table, and a dictionary on my shelf. Each of them had a red plastic label saying MARK TWO. Not long after, a pocket chess set arrived, and a toothbrush, and a poster of Manchester United. Each had a red label saying MARK TWO.

By mid-afternoon I was becoming seriously worried. One of the red plastic labels had appeared on my radio. Soon they were spreading like measles. By tea-time they had reached every single object in my room. I went down to complain to Mum and Dad, and found them giving Mark Two a front door key. Mark Two thanked them kindly and went off to do some shopping.

"Why did you give him a key?" I asked.

"How else can he open the door?" replied Dad.

Half an hour later Mark Two was back. He had a small paper package with him.

"I've bought something for our house," he said.

"*Our* house?" I replied.

"I hope everyone likes it," said Mark Two.

Mark Two carefully unwrapped the paper package. Inside was a small square of china. On this was a picture of a racing car and the words MARK'S ROOM.

"Where do you think you're putting that?" I asked.

"On the door, of course," replied Mark Two.

"Yes, but which door?" I asked.

"My door," replied Mark Two.

"I hope you don't mean *my* door," I warned him.

"I mean *my* door," said Mark Two.

With that, Mark Two began fixing the name-plate to my bedroom door. Boiling mad, I stamped downstairs to get Mum and Dad. "You've got to stop him!" I cried. "He's taking over!"

Mum and Dad looked at each other, deciding who would speak.

"Alex," said Mum, "there's something we have to tell you."

Dad put a fatherly hand on my shoulder. "Son," he said, "you're out of date."

"Out of date?" I gasped. "What do you mean?"

"We love you very much," said Mum, "but Mark Two is simply a better model."

"You can't blame us for wanting the best," said Dad.

I began to gently panic. "But ... what will happen to me?" I asked.

At this, Dad had a bad coughing attack and Mum remembered something in the oven.

Chapter 3

There was only one thing for it. I would have to prove that everything Mark Two could do, I could do better. Even if it meant washing my hair.

That evening, I put all my clothes on hangers and hung them in the wardrobe. Then I challenged Mark Two to a game of Brat Attack. No one had ever beaten me at Brat Attack, not even Jason Percy.

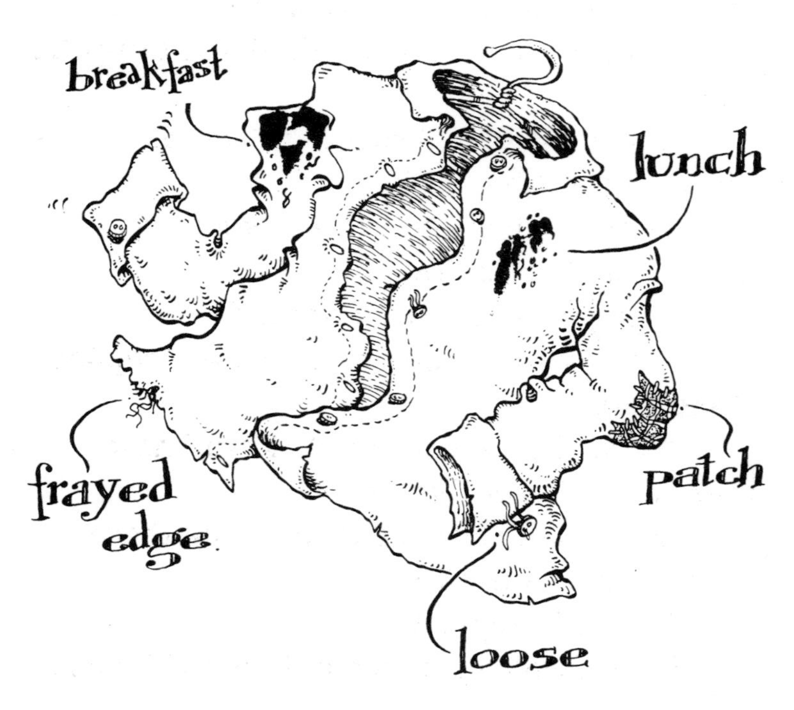

"Fifty-four's my record," I said proudly. "What's yours?"

Mark Two checked the name of the game, then flicked through his filofax.

"Six thousand, five hundred and thirty," he replied.

"Six thousand?" I sneered. "Liar! It doesn't go up that far!"

"It does when you get the bomb on board," said Mark Two.

"Bomb? I said. "What bomb?"

"You pick it up on Level Twelve," replied Mark Two.

"Level Twelve?" I said. "I never knew there was a Level Twelve."

"How many levels did you think there were?" asked Mark Two.

"Three," I replied.

Mark Two just smiled quietly to himself.

"Excellent," he said. "Let the contest begin."

I made an excuse about blowing up my air-bed and got out quick.

Half an hour later I was back.

"All right," I said. "How do you spell 'weather'?"

"'Weather' as in 'weather report' or 'whether' as in 'whether or not'?" asked Mark Two.

"OK, what's the capital of Bogmania?"

"There's no such country," replied Mark Two.

I wasn't finished yet. "I bet you can't rub your stomach and pat your head at the same time," I said.

I rubbed my stomach and patted my head. Mark Two rubbed his stomach, patted his head and drummed on his nose for good measure. I still don't know how he did it.

Just before bedtime, Dad came in. "Everything all right, Mark?" he asked.

"Fine, thank you," said Mark Two, "although the air-bed is rather inconvenient."

"We'll move it into the box-room," said Dad.

Next morning Pat and Phil called for me. Pat and Phil had been my mates for years. I hadn't told them about Mark Two, but they soon noticed him polishing Dad's shoes in the kitchen.

"Who's that?" asked Pat.

"What a wally!" said Phil.

My heart leapt. I had something Mark Two would never have – friends. Who'd be friends with someone that perfect? No one.

"Fancy a game of footy?" I asked.

"Sure," said Pat and Phil.

In seconds, Mark Two was at my shoulder. "May I play?" he asked.

I looked him coolly in the eyes. "I suggest you play with your own friends," I said.

There was a pause.

"But I've lost my address book," he said.

"Tough," I replied.

"It was in here somewhere," said Mark Two, reaching into his inside pocket. Suddenly there was a thud. Mark Two's wallet lay on the ground. It was stuffed full of fifty pound notes.

"Oops," said Mark Two. "Did I drop that?"

Mark Two picked up the wallet, drew it slowly past my friends' eyes, then lowered it back into his pocket.

"I've definitely lost my address book," said Mark Two. "Guess I'll have to make some new friends."

Two minutes later, Pat, Phil and Mark Two were playing football and I was packing up the shoe polish.

Later that day, I found Mark Two carrying a big pile of clothes to the washing machine.

"What's the matter?" he said. "Don't you do your own washing?"

I immediately fetched all my dirty clothes. "Of course I do my own washing," I said.

"What about everyone else's?" he asked.

With that Mark Two fetched Mum and Dad's washing as well.

"I think you've forgotten something," I said. I pulled all the sheets, pillowcases and duvet covers off the beds, and added them to my pile.

"Hmm," said Mark Two. "That's a start, anyway."

Mark Two set off round the house, taking down all the curtains, which he loaded on to his own pile. I then fetched the towels, Mark Two got the tea-towels, and we raced each other to pull the covers off the settee and the armchairs. That only left the tablecloths, the hankies and the dusters.

By now our piles were almost touching the ceiling.

"I hope this machine is the latest model," said Mark Two, as he loaded the first lot of washing in.

Hours passed, and the piles hardly seemed to get any smaller. It was dark before I took the very last load out of the tumble dryer. I flopped back into a chair, exhausted.

"Good," said Mark Two. "Now the ironing."

"Ironing?" I gasped.

"What's the matter?" said Mark Two. "Can't you iron?"

Mark Two set up an ironing board and started busily ironing away. Wearily, I dragged out the other ironing board and did the same. At first, I tried to keep up with Mark Two, but his arm moved so fast, you could hardly see it. Soon I was lagging well behind. Mark Two's pile was neat, crisp, and perfectly folded. Mine was all scorched and wrinkled.

My arm got slower and slower, heavier and heavier. The iron began to feel like a block of stone. Eventually I just had to stop.

"What's the matter?" said Mark Two. "Tired already?"

A little hiss of steam came out of Mark Two's iron. A hiss came from my ears too. I was furious.

"All right!" I snapped. "So you can iron! So you're good at computer games! So you're brainy! Well, let's see if you can *fight*!"

I leapt at Mark Two, fists whirling. I'm not sure what happened next. Somehow I ended up on the floor with my arms pinned behind me and Mark Two sitting triumphantly on top.

"That reminds me," said Mark Two. "I must iron my judo suit and black belt."

Chapter 4

Next morning, the box-room seemed even more cramped than before. I soon realized why. Mark Two had put my suitcases in there. Next to them were my wet-weather clothes, travel-sickness pills, and train timetables.

I rushed downstairs to find Mum and Dad.

"Mark Two's trying to kick me out!" I blurted.

"What makes you say that?" asked Mum.

I threw the train timetables on the floor. Mum and Dad looked at them for a while, then Dad carefully picked them up.

"Actually," said Dad, "I put those in your room."

My mouth dropped wide open.

"You did say you'd like a holiday," said Mum.

My lip quivered. "You're not sending me on holiday!" I blubbed. "You're getting rid of me!"

Mum and Dad could not deny it.

"Right!" I stormed. "I *will* go, then you'll be sorry!" I flung open the door. Just as I did so, a van appeared down the road. A big red van. It trundled up to our house and stopped outside. Two adults in track suits got out. They stretched a few times, then jogged up to the door.

"Is this Mark Two's house?" they asked.

"It's beginning to look that way," I replied.

"Excellent," they said. "We're his parents."

Mum and Dad seemed quite surprised.

"Parents?" said Dad. "We never knew Mark Two had parents."

"Everybody's got parents," replied the strange couple.

That was true enough.

"Well ..." said Mum. "You'd better come in."

The strange couple didn't need a second invitation. In a flash they were in the kitchen, running their eyes over the food supplies.

"I'm Marcia Two, by the way," said the woman, giving Dad a firm handshake.

"I'm Marcus," said the man, giving Mum an even firmer handshake.

Mark Two arrived. He was wearing a track suit, just like his mum and dad.

"Hello, Mark," said Marcia. "How are you settling in?"

"Very nicely, thank you, Mother," said Mark. He kissed his mother lightly on the cheek and gave his father a manly handshake.

Marcus checked his watch. "May we use your bathroom?" he asked.

Dad was puzzled. "All of you?" he asked.

"That's right," said Marcus.

"Well ... " said Dad, "I can't see why not."

"Thank you," said Marcus.

Marcia, Marcus and Mark Two jogged off to the bathroom in single file. Dad quickly closed the kitchen door.

"No one told us he had parents!" he whispered.

"I'm sure they'll go soon," said Mum.

Suddenly Mark Two's voice echoed through the house. "One! Two! Three! Four!" he chanted.

We decided to investigate. "Five! Six! Seven! Eight!" chanted Mark Two.

We arrived at the bathroom door. The Two family were side by side on the lino, doing press-ups. After fifty of these, they moved on to sit-ups, and after the sit-ups came chin-ups. They did the chin-ups on the curtain pole, which groaned and creaked and finally snapped in two, sending the Two family sprawling over the floor.

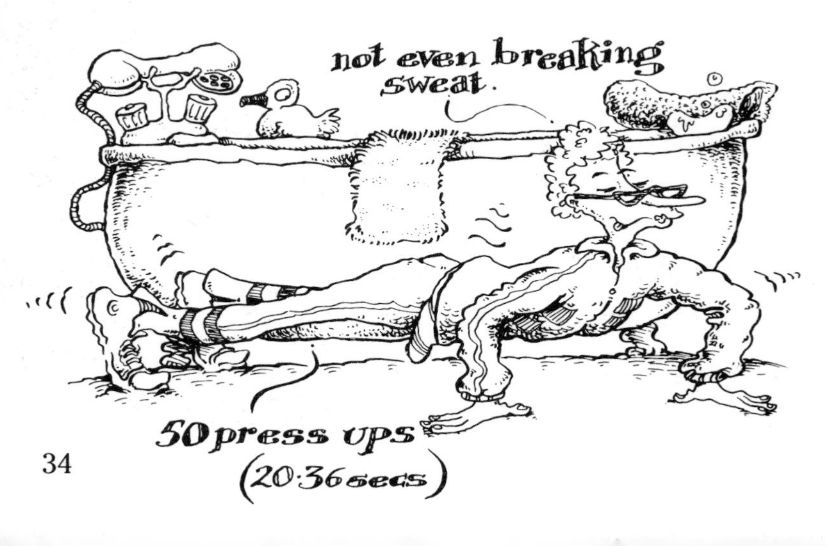

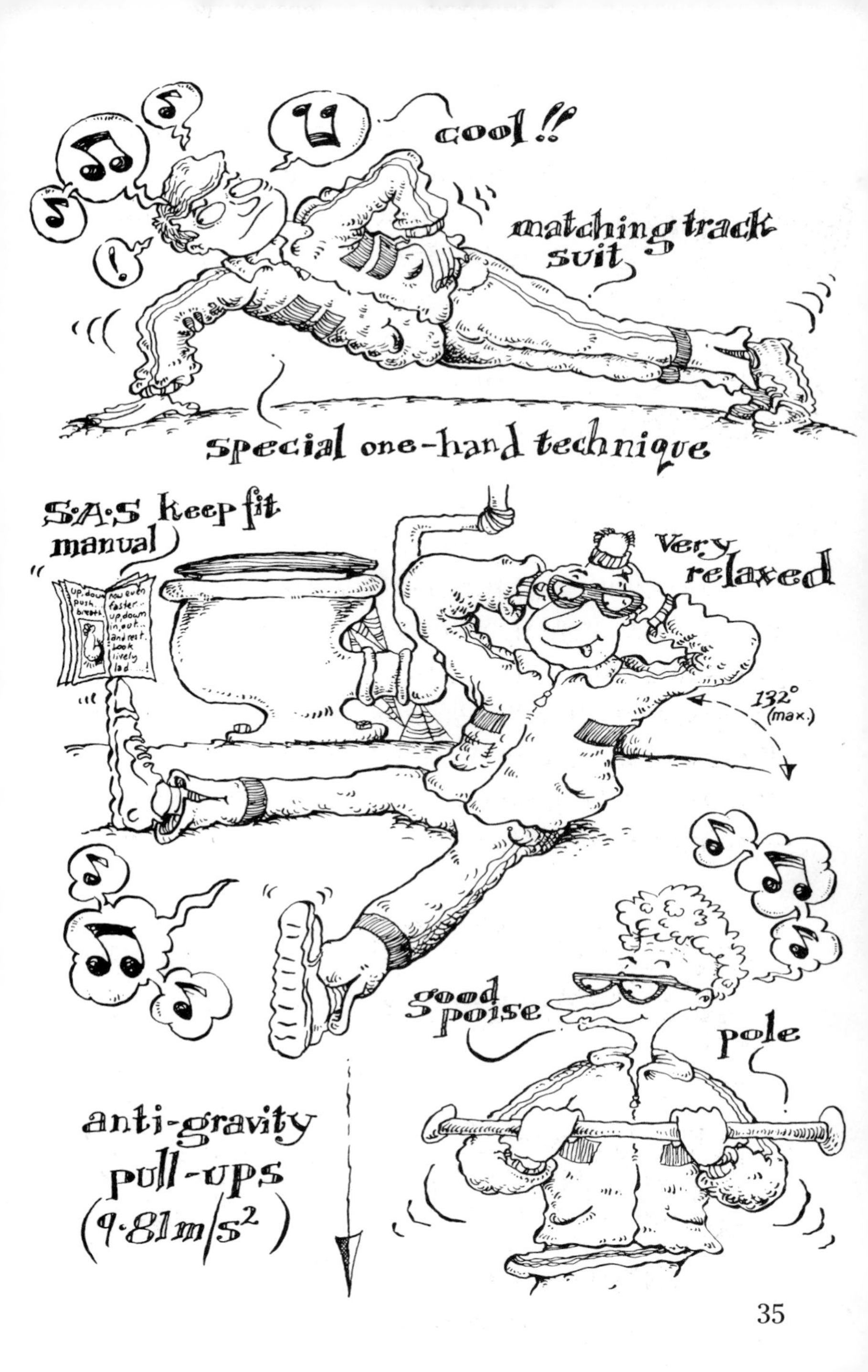
cool!!
matching track suit
special one-hand technique
S·A·S keep fit manual
up, down push.. breath..
now even faster.. up, down in, out.. and rest. Look lively lad
very relaxed
132° (max.)
good poise
pole
anti-gravity pull-ups (9·81m/s²)

"My curtain pole!" cried Mum.

"Awfully sorry," said Marcus.

"We'll get a new one tomorrow," said Marcia.

When they had finished their exercises, Marcia and Marcus checked Mark's homework, and the stories he had written, and the computer program he had invented.

"Well done, Mark," said Marcus. "Your work is excellent, as always."

"Thank you, Father," said Mark. "And thank you, also, for spending so much time with me."

"Not at all," said Marcus.

"And remember," said Marcia, "if you have any problems, tell us straight away, so we can discuss them openly and honestly, like good parents should."

"Very well," said Mark. "I would like more pocket money."

"Of course," said Marcus. He took out a huge, fat wallet stuffed with notes and gave Mark Two fifty pounds.

"Thank you, Father," said Mark. "I shall put it straight in my savings account."

Mum and Dad watched all this as if it was a film on the telly. Now and then Mum checked her watch. Marcus and Marcia showed no signs of leaving.

"Goodness, I'm tired!" said Marcia, suddenly. "I wonder if I might have a lie down?"

"Well ..." said Mum, "you could use our room, I suppose."

"Bad move, Mum!" I whispered, but Marcia had already thanked Mum and left the room.

Chapter 5

Mum slept on the sofa that night. Dad had a few cushions on the floor.

I was woken at seven o'clock by loud conversation. I crawled down to the kitchen, where I found the Two family sitting down to a slap-up breakfast. Marcia had a large, difficult-looking newspaper and was testing Mark Two on the news. Marcus was looking round the room and making little notes and sketches.

"This really is a nice kitchen," said Marcus.

"Yes," agreed Marcia. "It will look lovely in yellow."

After breakfast, the Two family did the washing up together. Marcus washed, Mark dried, and Marcia stood with a stopwatch screaming, "Go! Go! Go!" By the time Mum and Dad got up, the kitchen was perfect, and the Two family had gone off to town.

This was our big chance. All we had to do was change the locks, bar the windows, and dig a moat round the house.

Mum and Dad, however, would have none of it.

"One doesn't throw one's guests out on the street," said Mum. "It simply isn't done."

"Besides," said Dad, "they're getting us a new curtain pole."

When the Twos did come back, they had at least twenty shopping bags. The curtain pole was poking out of one of the bags. Rolls of wallpaper were sticking out of another.

Marcus handed Mum the curtain pole. He said it was the latest model and completely unbreakable.

"We've also bought you a little present," said Marcia.

"Oh!" said Dad, blushing. "Thank you!"

Marcia handed Dad a package, which looked like a huge sausage. Dad unwrapped it. Inside was a long, fat nylon bag.

"It's ... a tent," said Dad.

"We hope you like the colour," said Marcia.

"Um ..." said Dad.

"Er ..." said Mum.

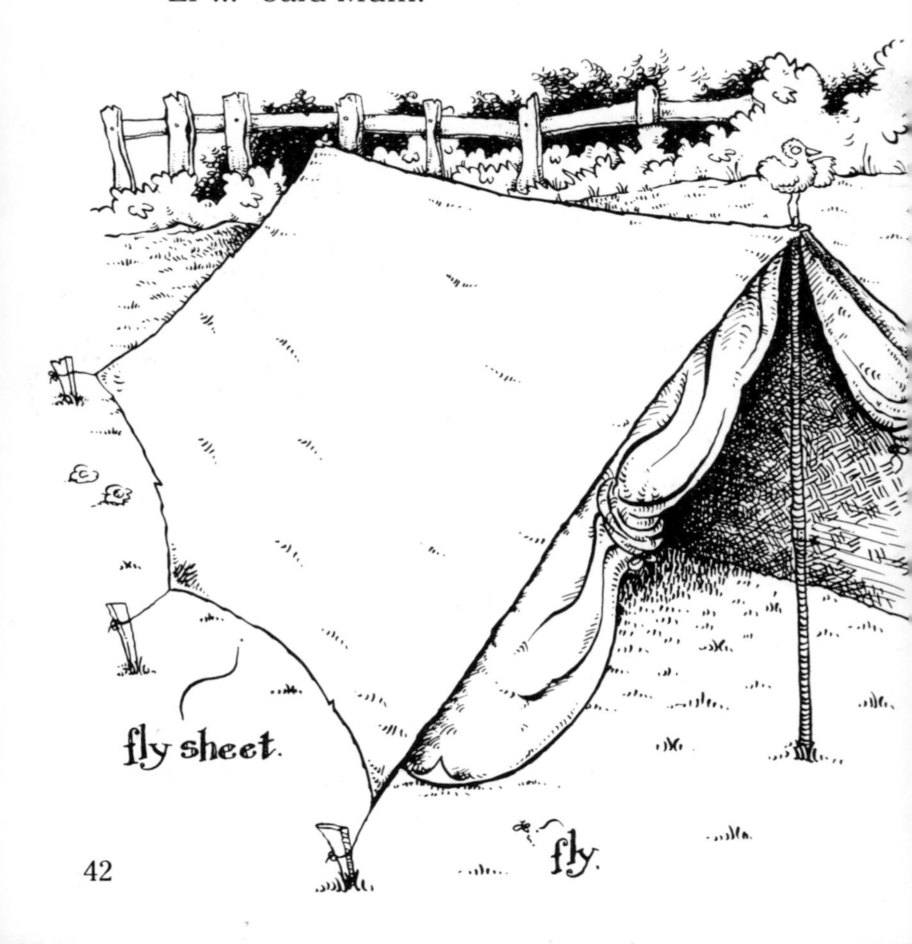

Marcia took the tent and quickly organized the other Twos. We watched, speechless, as they set to work on the back lawn. This time it was Mark and Marcia's turn to work, while Marcus held the stopwatch and went, "Go! Go! Go!" The tent was up in no time, and we were invited to inspect it.

"I love the outdoor life," said Marcus. "Don't you?"

"Not really," said Mum.

Marcus didn't seem to hear her. "Right," he said. "You just get yourselves settled in there, and we'll fetch your stuff."

Mum and Dad were speechless. The Two family jogged back to the house, and a moment later the light went on in Mum and Dad's room. The Two family busily collected the bedding, the bedside books, and the bits and pieces off the dressing table.

"*Now* will you listen to me?" I said.

"But this is all wrong!" said Dad. "We only ordered Mark Two, not his parents!"

"Well, now you know how I feel," I said.

Mum and Dad decided they would sort the matter out right away. When the Two family came back, Mum and Dad stood across the door of the tent.

"Halt!" said Dad.

"Take our belongings back this minute!" said Mum.

"I beg your pardon?" said Marcia, confused.

"If you think you've moving in," said Dad, "you are very much mistaken!"

The Two family stood their ground. They were not shaken in the least.

"Of course we're moving in," said Marcia.

"We've been as nice about it as possible," said Marcus.

"Now listen here!" said Mum. "We only ordered Mark Two, not you as well!"

Marcia shook her head. "You obviously didn't read the small print," she said. "We come as a set."

"You can't have one of us," said Marcus, "without having all of us."

It was just as I had expected.

"But ... *we* want to be Mark Two's parents," said Dad.

"Don't be silly," said Mark Two. "There's no point in getting a new CD player and putting it with old speakers!"

The Two family laughed loudly at Mark Two's joke. They put Mum and Dad's gear in the tent and went off to start decorating.

Chapter 6

What could we do? We couldn't go to the police, because the Twos hadn't done anything wrong. We couldn't fight them, and we certainly couldn't outsmart them. We just had to grin and bear it.

It didn't take the Twos long to change the house completely. They changed the furniture, the wallpaper, the carpets and the cupboards.

They knocked the living-room through into the dining-room, built a gym in the attic, and made a workshop in the shed. They also put a sign up outside the house saying "La Casa Due".

It was French, or Spanish, or something. The Twos liked to speak in foreign languages. Even when they spoke English we couldn't understand them, because they used such long words.

The more we saw of the Twos, the more useless we felt. There didn't seem any point in doing anything. The Twos could always do it better.

One evening, the Twos held a party for all the neighbours. Marcus set up a de-luxe barbecue in the back garden. Mark Two served champagne. Marcia entertained on the guitar. We sat in the middle of it all, cooking a tin of beans on the camping stove. Everyone tried to pretend we weren't there.

After the guests had gone, Marcus and Marcia had a quiet word with each other.

"It was a very nice party," said Marcia, "but it wasn't quite perfect."

"I agree," said Marcus. "We shall have to get rid of that tent."

Next morning there was a strange atmosphere in the house. When we came in to get our cornflakes, the Twos were sitting silently round the kitchen table.

“Marcia finally spoke. “The blue van,” she said, “is coming today.”

“Blue van?” repeated Mum, nervously.

“Is that like the red van?” asked Dad, even more nervously.

“Not exactly,” said Marcia.

There was another silence.

“The blue van,” said Marcus, “is the second-hand van.”

“From the second-hand warehouse,” added Marcia.

“I’m not sure what you mean,” said Mum.

“As you know,” said Marcus, “when you buy a new cooker, they usually take the old one away for you.”

"It's called 'part exchange'," said Mark Two with a smarty-pants smile.

"Oh," said Dad. "Are you getting a new cooker?"

Marcus coughed. "I don't think you quite understand," he said.

"The blue van," said Marcia, "is coming for *you*."

A numb feeling came over me. I thought of putting tin-tacks in the road. I thought of chaining myself to the kitchen sink. There was no way I was going in the blue van.

Mark Two, however, had other ideas. He found my toothbrush and put my travel-sickness pills and wet weather clothes in a bag. He even rolled up my Manchester City poster, which was the only thing left without a red label on it.

"I'd get myself ready," he said, "if I were you."

"Well you're not me, are you?" I snapped.

"No," said Mark Two. "Certainly not."

Mark Two went out. For a moment I felt angry. Then, suddenly, I had a flash of genius. Mark Two had given me an idea, an idea which might save us from the dreaded blue van.

Chapter 7

Later that morning I walked into the living-room with Mum and Dad. The Twos thought we had come to say goodbye. They had another think coming.

"We have decided," I said, "that you are not as good as us."

Marcus laid down his difficult book. "Oh yes?" he said. "And why is that?"

"Because," I said, "there is something we can do better."

Marcia smiled calmly. "Oh yes?" she said. "And what is that?"

"Acting," I replied.

"Acting?" said Mark Two. "We're brilliant at acting!"

The Two family jumped smartly to their feet and paced round the room, doing Shakespeare very loudly.

"Not that kind of acting," I said.

"Then what kind?" asked Mark Two, still in his loud Shakespeare voice.

"The kind where we pretend to be you, and you pretend to be us."

"Oh," said Mark Two. "Im-pro-vis-ation."

"If you say so," I replied.

"Well," said Mark Two. "Let's see, shall we?"

We handed the Twos a bag of our clothes. Then we went off and put on their track suits. A few minutes later we jogged back into the room and started doing press-ups. By now the Twos were dressed as us. They sat around looking gormless.

"One, two, three, four!" I yelled, as Mum and Dad did their sit-ups.

"Go! Go! Go!" said Mum, as Dad and I dusted the shelves. But the better we acted, the better the Twos acted. They were so good, I almost believed they were us.

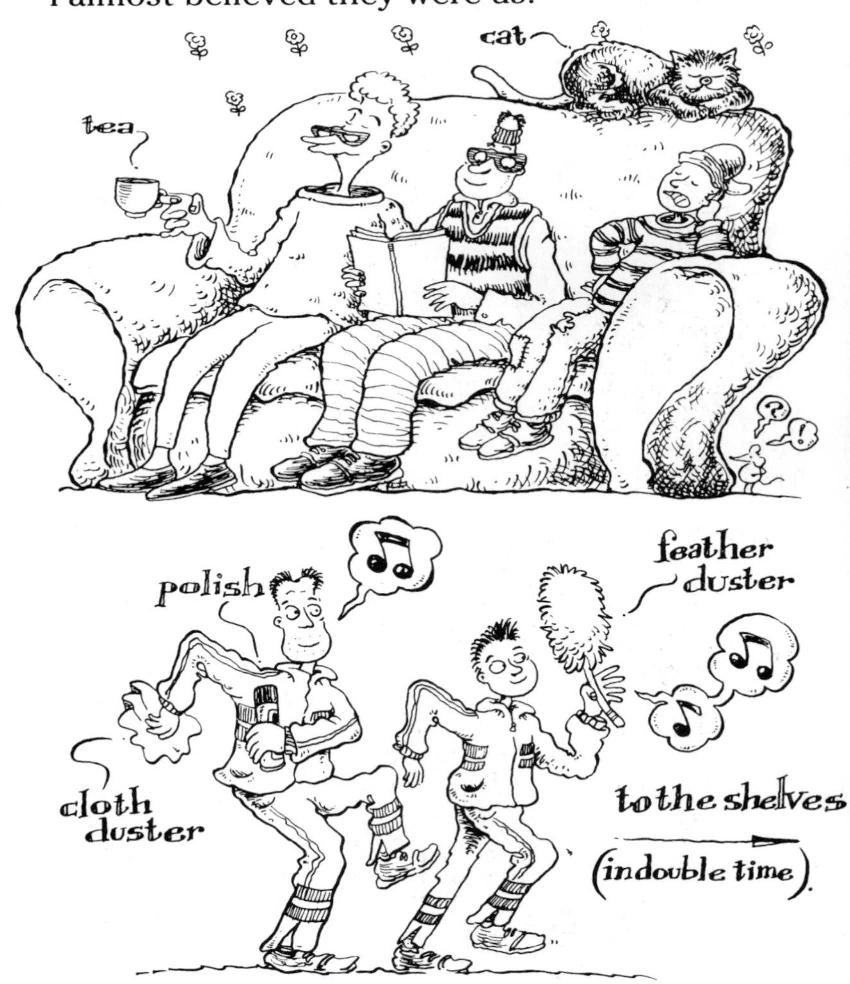

This went on for ten minutes or so. Then there was the sound of an engine, a few blocks away. Not long after, a blue van turned into our road.

The Two family saw nothing of the van. They were so carried away, they had gone out into the back garden to cook a tin of beans. I don't think they even heard the doorbell go.

"Got some second-hand stuff for us?" said the removal man.

"In the back garden," replied Mum.

"Thanks very much, Mrs Two," said the removal man.

Six more men came out of the blue van. They all went out the back. We heard a lot of shouting, and swearing, and scuffling noises. Then Marcus, Marcia and Mark were marched back through the house.

"This is intolerable," said Marcus.

"Inexcusable," said Marcia.

"Scandalous," said Mark.

We waved the Twos a cheery farewell. "Bye, Alex!" I shouted, but Mark never got the chance to reply. All three were bundled into the blue van, and the engine roared into life. We caught one last glimpse of the Twos, faces pressed against the rear windows. Then they were gone.

Mum and Dad sighed with relief.

"It's all over now," said Dad.

"Thanks to Alex," said Mum.

Mum gave me a hug. Dad looked a little embarrassed. "You know," he said, "I never *really* preferred Mark Two."

Mum agreed. "There's a lot to be said for the older models," she said.

There was an awkward silence.

"You will forgive us, won't you?" said Dad.

I thought about it. "All right," I said, "but on one condition."

"Yes?" said Mum and Dad, together.

"You must promise," I said, "never to get me a Titan Superthrust Mark 2."

Mum and Dad looked disappointed. "We were going to buy you one tomorrow," said Dad.

“It’s the least you deserve,” said Mum.

I wagged my finger sternly. “No, Mum and Dad,” I said. “You are *not* to buy me that bike. In fact, you are not to buy me the latest *anything*.”

“Well ... if you say so,” said Dad, doubtfully.

“I do say so,” I replied.

Mum and Dad accepted that I meant it. I left the house and went for a walk, feeling as if a great weight had been lifted from me.

Just round the corner, who should I see but my old rival Jason Percy. He was sitting in the gutter with his head in his hands.

"What's up, Jase?" I said, cheerfully.

"They've brought out a Titan Supercharge Mark 3," said Jason. "Lynnette Smith's got one."

"Wouldn't worry about it, mate," I said.